A Persian Princess

By Barbara Diamond Goldin • Illustrated by Steliyana Doneva

APPLES & HONEY PRESS

To my granddaughter Hanna, who loves princesses,
and to Miriam Levy-Haim and her family, including
the real Nati, for all their help in the writing of this book
—B.D.G.

To all grandmothers (like Maman)
who preserve their family values —S.D.

Persian Jews use different words for "grandmother."
Maman, *Maman joon*, *Maman Borzog*, and *Mamany*, are
some of these. *Maman* means "mother." *Joon* means
"life, breath, soul" and is an endearment.

The illustrations in this book were sketched on paper
and enhanced using digital techniques.

Apples & Honey Press
An imprint of Behrman House
Millburn, New Jersey 07041
www.applesandhoneypress.com

Text copyright © 2020 Barbara Diamond Goldin
Illustrations copyright © 2020 Steliyana Doneva
Artwork for border pattern on page 32: Shutterstock, Architaste
ISBN 978-1-68115-553-1

Library of Congress Cataloging-in-Publication Data

Names: Goldin, Barbara Diamond, author. | Doneva, Steliyana, illustrator.
Title: A Persian princess : by Barbara Diamond Goldin ;
illustrated by Steliyana Doneva.
Description: Millburn, New Jersey : Apples and Honey Press, [2020] | Summary:
"A grandmother shares stories with her granddaughter about how she used to
celebrated Purim in the old country, Iran"—Provided by publisher.
Identifiers: LCCN 2019002820 | ISBN 9781681155531
Subjects: LCSH: Purim—Iran—Juvenile fiction.
Classification: LCC PZ7.G5674 Per 2020 | DDC [E]—dc23
LC record available at https://lccn.loc.gov/2019002820

Design by Elynn Cohen
Edited and art directed by Ann D. Koffsky
Printed in China

2 4 6 8 9 7 5 3 1

0222/B1847/A6

Raya sprinkled more flour into the cookie dough and kneaded it.
She couldn't wait to eat the Purim cookies, the *koloocheh*.
"I'm going to make some hearts from the dough," said Raya.

"Good. I'll shape ones that look like little men," said her grandmother, Maman joon.

"The Haman cookies?" asked Raya.

"Yes!" said Maman joon. "When I was a girl in Hamadan, in Iran, we pretended the cookies were Haman, the king's mean counselor. When the cookies come out of the oven soon—crunch!—we'll eat the Hamans all up!"

Raya giggled.

Just then Raya's big brother Nati burst into the kitchen.
"Anyone have scissors? My beard is way too long," he said.
"Who are you supposed to be?" asked Maman joon.

"Mordecai in the religious school play, Queen Esther's cousin."

"I wish I could be in the play," said Raya.

Maman joon looked at Raya. "Don't worry. You'll be in a play next year."

"It's not fair," said Raya. "I have to wait for everything."

Maman joon cut Nati's beard and put safety pins all around the bottom of their father's bathrobe so Nati could walk without tripping. Suddenly there were some loud knocks on the front door.

"That's Danny," said Nati. "I have to hurry or we'll miss the rehearsal."

Raya watched Nati run off.

"Don't look so glum," said Maman joon. "Soon the cookies will be ready."

"But I can't be in the play this year. And Mom hasn't even made my Purim costume yet."

"Did you tell her what you want to be?"

"A princess with a sparkly dress."

"Hmmm," said Maman joon. "Come with me, my sweet Raya joon. I have just the thing."

Raya followed her grandmother up the stairs.

At the top, Maman joon pushed open the door to her room.

There were colorful Persian rugs on the floor, a shiny golden tea set on the bureau, and rich smells, sweet and spicy.

Her grandmother walked over to an old trunk with gold and silver jewelry and red, purple, pink, and green scarves that sparkled in the light.

"Maman joon!" Raya whispered.

"I saved these from Hamadan. We wore them on special days."

Maman joon pulled scarf after scarf from the trunk and draped them over Raya, even over her hair. They were silky, with silver and golden threads woven in. Then Maman joon covered Raya with strands of gold coins sewn together that tinkled when Raya moved.

"Maman joon, you'll really let me wear these?"

"It would make me happy if you wore them. They remind me of people and places I miss."

"Then I'll be a Persian princess!" said Raya.
Maman joon nodded. "How perfect!"

"Did you know that the story of Purim took place in Persia, close to where I grew up? That's why people came to celebrate Purim with us. Such fun we had then." Maman joon's eyes welled up with tears.

Raya hugged her grandmother, and they both went downstairs, where sweet, warm smells filled the air. The cookies were done!

Raya filled boxes for each of their neighbors with cookies. She and Maman joon carried them out the door.

"When I was a girl, we brought sweets to our neighbors, too," said Maman joon.

First, they knocked on Mrs. Levy's door. When she answered, Mrs. Levy put her hands on her face in delight. "Oh! Purim treats for us? And what a beautiful costume!" she cried.

"I'm a Persian princess," said Raya.

Raya gave Mrs. Levy's little girl Ora a box and told her how Esther was Persian, just like their families were.

"She was such a brave queen, Ora," Raya said. "She saved her people from the wicked Haman!"

"Tell more," said Ora.

"Mordecai told Esther about Haman's plot. And she went before the king even though she was afraid."

"More story," Ora said again.

Raya grew quiet, thinking.

"Maman joon, what if we invite Ora and all the children in the neighborhood to our house? I could tell them the Purim story. Maybe we could even put on a play."

"That's my Raya joon," said her grandmother.

"Then I won't have to wait to be in a play! Mrs. Levy, can Ora come to our house later?" asked Raya.

"Of course," said Mrs. Levy, and Ora clapped her hands.

Raya and Maman joon walked to each neighbor's
house, delivering boxes and inviting everyone to the play.

Walking back home, Raya told Maman joon, "I can be Esther. This costume is good for a princess or a queen. You can be the king. Nati can be Mordecai. And for Haman we can use one of your cookies."

"Nati will like that," said Maman joon with a smile.

Raya was so excited, she skipped the rest of the way home, but not too fast. She didn't want to leave Maman joon behind.

They had so much to do to get ready.

In the living room, Raya and her grandmother cleared a space for a stage. Maman joon brought down rugs and even the golden tea set from her room. The stage looked like a room in the king's palace.

Maman joon put on a fancy robe. "My father's," she explained. She made a crown of gold paper and a beard from brown fabric.

"You don't look like Maman joon anymore," joked Raya.

Then Raya heard people coming down the street.

"It's the neighbors," Raya called. "And Nati, Mom, and Dad are just in time."

"Nati, don't take off your costume," said Maman joon when he came in the house.

Soon everyone was sitting around the stage.

"Here we are in the king's palace," began Raya.
"I pick you, Esther, to be my queen," said the king.
"Haman plans to destroy us just because I won't bow
down to him!" said Mordecai. "I have to get word to Esther."

Even though it was dangerous, Esther bravely approached the king. "Please, dear king. Spare my people," she asked him. The king took Esther's hand and said, "I will change Haman's decree. Your people are saved."

The guests, young and old, clapped and whistled and shook their noisemakers. And a happy Ora did too!

Raya cuddled up next to her grandmother.
"Are you happy, Maman joon? Everyone came
to our house for Purim just like when you lived
in Hamadan."

"It's even better now, Raya joon.
I have my little Persian princess
here, too."

A Note for Families

The story of Purim is found in the biblical book of Esther, and the setting is ancient Persia (now Iran). The king, Achashverosh, chooses a new queen named Esther, who is Jewish but keeps her religion a secret. Trouble begins when the king's advisor, Haman, becomes angry with Mordecai, who will not bow down to him. Haman plots to kill Mordecai and all the Jews in the kingdom. Mordecai warns Esther, who risks her life to speak to the king about Haman's plot and thus saves the Jews.

Jews have lived in the area that is now Iran for over twenty-five hundred years. Before 1979, there were about eighty thousand Jews in Iran. To celebrate Purim, many would come to the city of Hamadan, where Maman joon is from, because according to tradition, the tombs of Mordecai and Esther are located there. They would visit the tombs, where they would chant the story of Esther. They would also bake special Purim cookies called *koloocheh* and shared baskets of food, called *mishloach manot*, with relatives and friends.

Then, in 1979 there was great unrest in Iran. The climate for the Jews changed, and about two-thirds of them left Iran and settled in other countries, including the United States. Today, the largest communities of Persian Jews in the United States are in Los Angeles, California, and Great Neck, New York. Jewish people there continue their traditions and celebrate Purim by making and giving treats to family, friends, and the poor and by sharing the story of Esther and Mordecai, just like Raya and her family.